ROTHERHAM PUBLIC LIBRARIES

What's That Noise?

What's That Noise?

Francesca Simon · David Melling

Hodder
Children's
Books

a division of Hodder Headline plc

One night Harry went to sleep
at Grandpa and Grandma's house.

For the first time in his life, Harry slept
in a strange bed
in a strange room.

It was very dark.

Suddenly Harry heard a strange noise.

SPUTTER-CLICK SPUTTER-CLICK
WHOOOSH!

"Grandpa, Grandpa, come quickly!" shouted Harry.
"What's that noise?"

Grandpa ran upstairs to Harry's room.

No noise here.

No noise there.

No noise anywhere.

Then suddenly . . .

"Harry it's only the radiator.
Now snuggle down and go to sleep."

Everything was quiet until . . .

NEE NAW NEE NAW

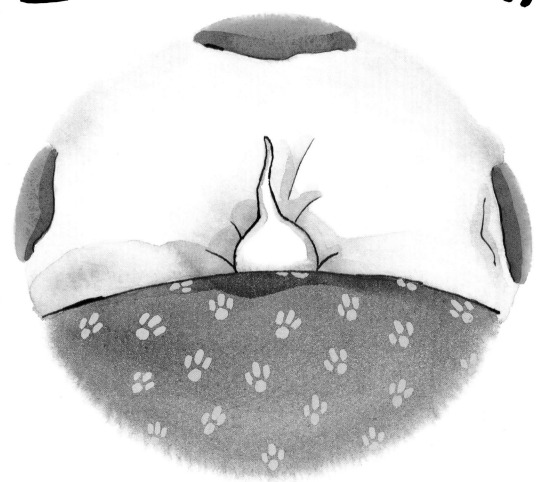

"Grandpa, Grandpa, come quickly!
What's that noise?"

"Harry, it's only . . .

a fire engine.

Now snuggle down and go to sleep."

Everything was quiet again until . . .

RUMBLE **RUMBLE** **RUMBLE**

"Grandpa, Grandpa, come quickly!
What's that noise?"

"Harry, it's only . . .

an aeroplane.

RUMBLE RUMBLE VRO

Now snuggle down and go to sleep."

Everything was quiet until . . .

"Grandpa, Grandpa, come quickly!
What's that noise?"

"Harry, it's only . . .

Mrs Ruffle next door
hammering.

Now snuggle down and go to sleep."

For a while everything was quiet.
Grandpa settled down in his comfy bed
and read his book.

Suddenly he heard a
strange snuffling noise.

snuffle   snuffle

"Grandma, Grandma, come quickly!
What's that noise?"

"I don't know," said Grandma.

They heard the snuffling rustling again,
only this time it was louder.

"I think the noise is coming from Harry's room," whispered Grandma.

Grandma and Grandpa
tiptoed up the stairs
to the attic.

The snuffling noise
got closer . . .

. . . and closer

Slowly Grandma opened
Harry's door.

"Grandpa, it's only Harry snuffling and snoring.

Now snuggle down and go to sleep."

For Joshua and his grandparents:
Sondra and Mayo Simon,
Owen and Hugh Stamp - FC.

For Tanja - DM.

A catalogue record of this book is available from the British Library

ISBN 0 340 65592 5   HB
ISBN 0 340 65673 5   PB

Text copyright © Francesca Simon 1996
Illustrations copyright © David Melling 1996
Designed by Rowan Seymour

First edition published 1996

10 9 8 7 6 5 4 3 2 1

Published by Hodder Children's Books
a division of Hodder Headline plc,
338 Euston Road, London NW1 3BH

Printed in Hong Kong.